The Rabbits' Rebellion

www.booksattransworld.co.uk/childrens

ARIEL DORFMAN

Illustrated by Chris Riddell

DOUBLEDAY

TRANSWORLD PUBLISHERS
61–63 Uxbridge Road, London W5 5SA
A division of The Random House Group Ltd

RANDOM HOUSE AUSTRALIA (PTY) LTD
20 Alfred Street, Milsons Point, Sydney
New South Wales 2061, Australia

RANDOM HOUSE NEW ZEALAND LTD
18 Poland Road, Glenfield, Auckland 10, New Zealand

RANDOM HOUSE (PTY) LTD
Endulini, 5A Jubilee Road, Parktown 2193, South Africa

Originally published in the USA by J B Lipincott Junior Books,
in *Where Angels Glide at Dawn*
First publication in Great Britain

Published in 2001 by Doubleday
A division of Transworld Publishers

1 3 5 7 9 10 8 6 4 2

A catalogue record for this book is available
from the British Library.

ISBN 0 385 601263

Typeset by
Phoenix Typesetting, Ilkley, West Yorkshire

Printed in Great Britain by
Mackays of Chatham plc, Chatham, Kent

When the wolves conquered the land of the rabbits, the first thing the leader of the pack did was to proclaim himself king. The second was to announce that the rabbits had ceased to exist. Now and for ever it would be forbidden to even mention their name.

Just to be on the safe side, the new Wolf King went over every book in his realm with a big black pencil, crossing out words and tearing out pictures of cottontails until he was satisfied that not a trace of his enemies remained.

But an old grey fox who was his counsellor brought bad news.

"The birds, Your Wolfiness, insist that they have seen some . . . some of those creatures. From on high."

"So how come I don't see anything from way up here, on my throne?" asked the wolf.

"In times like these," answered the fox, "people have got to see to believe."

"Seeing is believing? Bring me that monkey

who takes photos, the one who lives nearby. I'll teach those birds a lesson."

The monkey was old and weak. "What can the Wolf of all Wolves want with me?" he asked, looking at his wife and daughter.

The little girl had an answer. "He must want you to take a picture of the rabbits, Dad."

"Quiet, quiet," said her mother. "Rabbits don't exist."

But the little monkey knew that rabbits did exist. It was true that, since the howling wolves had invaded the country, the rabbits no longer came to visit her as they had before. But in her dreams she continued hearing the green rain of their voices singing nearby, reflecting in her head as if she were a pond under the moonlight, and when she awoke there was always

a small gift beside her bed. Walls and closed doors were like water for the rabbits.

"That's why I sleep well," said the little girl. "That's why that General Wolf must need the photo. To keep nightmares away. You'll bring me a picture of them someday, won't you, Dad?"

The monkey felt fear crawl up and down his fur. "Send this little girl to her room," he told his wife, "until she understands that there are certain things we just don't talk about."

The King of the Wolves was not in the best of moods when the monkey came in. "You're late. And I'm in a hurry. I need photographs of each important act in my life. And all my acts, let me tell you, are supremely important . . . Can you guess what we're going to do with those pictures? You can't? We're going to put one on every street, inside every bush, in every home. I'll be there, watching each citizen with my very own eyes. You'd better pity those who don't have the latest events of my life hung up on their walls. And you know who is going to distribute each picture? You don't know?"

The monkey was trembling so hard that no words came out.

"The birds, ugly monkey. Now they'll bite their own beaks before they twitter around with any nonsense about rabbits. And we'll tie an endless cord to their legs, so they can't escape. Understand?"

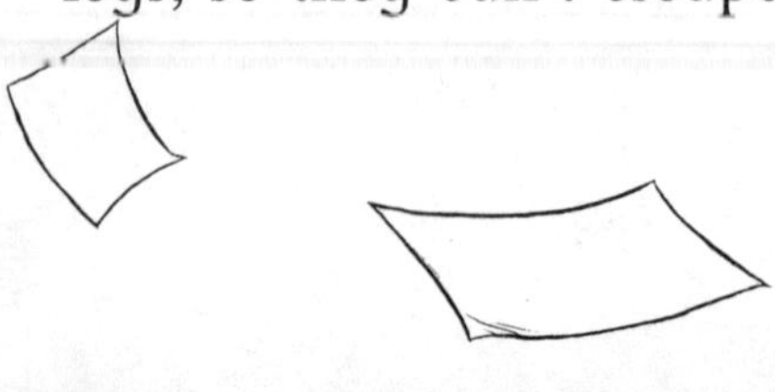

The monkey understood so well that his trembling paw immediately clicked the shutter of the camera, taking the first picture.

"Go," roared the Wolf, "and develop it. I want it on every wall in the kingdom."

But when the photographer returned some minutes later, he did not dare to enter the throne room, and asked one of the soldiers to call the counsellor. Without a word, the monkey passed him the picture he had just taken.

The fox blinked once, and then blinked again. In a corner of the photo, far from the muscular, ferocious figure of

the King – who had both arms up in the air as if he had just won a boxing championship – appeared what was without any doubt the beginning of an ear, the ear of someone who had insolently come to spy on the whole ceremony.

"You blind monkey!" fumed the fox. "How come you didn't notice that this . . . this thing was there? Can't you focus that camera of yours?"

"If it could get into the picture," the monkey answered, "it was because you and your guards let it get close."

"It won't happen again," the counsellor promised. "Rub out that . . . ear before His Wolfishness finds out."

From his bag, the monkey took out a special liquid that he used to erase any detail that might bother a client. The intruding ear began to disappear as if it had never existed.

The King of the Wolves was pleased with the portrait and ordered it sent all over the realm. Two hours later he

personally went on an inspection tour to make sure that not a window was without a picture of his large, gleaming, dangerous grin. "Not bad," he said, "but this photo is already getting old. People should see my latest deeds. Take another. Quick. Show me scaring these pigeons – right away. And bring it to me immediately. You took too long last time."

But the monkey wasn't able to comply this time either. Once again he had the counsellor called secretly.

"Again?" asked the fox. "It happened again?"

Except that now it was worse than an indiscreet ear. A whole corner of the new picture was filled with the unmistakable face of . . . yes, there was no denying it, of a rabbit winking an eye in open defiance of the nearby guards.

"We've got to tighten security," muttered the fox.

"Meanwhile, erase that invader."

"Wonderful," shouted the King Wolf when he was finally given the picture. "Look at the frightened faces of the pigeons trying to escape. I want a million copies. I want them on milk cartons and on the coupons inside cereals . . . Onwards. Onwards. Let's go and smash up a dam. Come on, monkey. Fame awaits us both."

The beavers had been working summer and winter for three years on a beautiful dam that would allow them to irrigate a distant valley.

The Wolf of Wolves climbed a tree. "I want you to shoot the precise moment when my feet crash into the middle of the dam, monkey. If you miss the shot, next time I'll fall on top of you and then I'll have to get myself another photographer. Are you ready?"

Not only was the monkey ready, so was the counsellor. The fox was breathing down the old monkey's back, peering over his shoulder, watching, listening. Nothing could escape those vigilant, darting eyes. Not a fuzzy ear would dare to make its appearance.

So neither the monkey nor the fox could believe it when, a bit later, they saw at the bottom of the picture a rabbit lolling on his side as if he were relaxing at a picnic. Next to him, another rabbit had raised her paw and was boldly thumbing her nose.

"This is an epidemic," said the fox. "And let me tell you, our lives are in danger."

"Let's start erasing," the monkey said wearily.

"You erase. I'll get a squadron of buzzards and hawks. They see all animals, even the quick and the small."

His Wolfhood the King yelped with pleasure when he saw a picture. It portrayed him at the exact moment he was breaking the backbone of the beavers' dam. In the distance, families of beavers could be seen fleeing. There was not a single shadow of a rabbit.

"Send it out! A strong country is an educated country, a country that always is tuned in to the latest news. What are we going to do now for some fun?"

"We could rest," the monkey suggested, his paws peeling from the harsh erasing fluid.

The Wolf looked at him as if he were a stone.

"And who asked you for an opinion? I'm in charge here. That's why I was born with these teeth, and you'd better pray you never have to feel them crunching your bones. Onwards. We are the future, the morrow, the dawn! We'll go on until there's no more light."

But in each new photo, the rabbits became more plentiful, audacious and saucy. His Wolfinity the King destroyed sugar mills, shook squirrels out of their trees and hid their nuts, stripped ducks of their feathers, drove sheep off cliffs, drilled holes in the road so that horses

would break their legs, unveiled new cages and old dungeons . . . and the more his frightening yellow eyes flickered, the more innumerable were the rabbits of every colour that frolicked in the margins of the photographs. Even the clouds seemed full of fur and whiskers and cottontails.

"Hey, birdie," jeered the Supreme Wolf, grabbing a swallow about to fly off with a bag overflowing with pictures, "what tune are you singing now, featherhead? Who's that in the centre of the picture, huh? Who's the King?"

The bird held his beak tight, so that not even a peep could come out.

"Lights, camera, action, monkey!" the Monarch demanded. "Call this: WOLF KING RECEIVES HOMAGE FROM A MESSENGER."

The monkey obeyed, but could hardly hide his despair. Though nobody ever saw the rebels when the photos were taken, they were always there when it was time to show them, nibbling lettuce at the very feet of the biggest and baddest of wolves.

"Exterminate them," hissed the fox, who had ordered a stronger, more acid liquid. "Don't leave even a twitch of a nose."

But the pictures were beginning to look defective. There were blank spaces everywhere. The monkey knew that the only solution was to convince His Wolfiness to sit up high on an elevated

throne. Since rabbits live underground, they wouldn't be able to wiggle their way into the frame of the photograph.

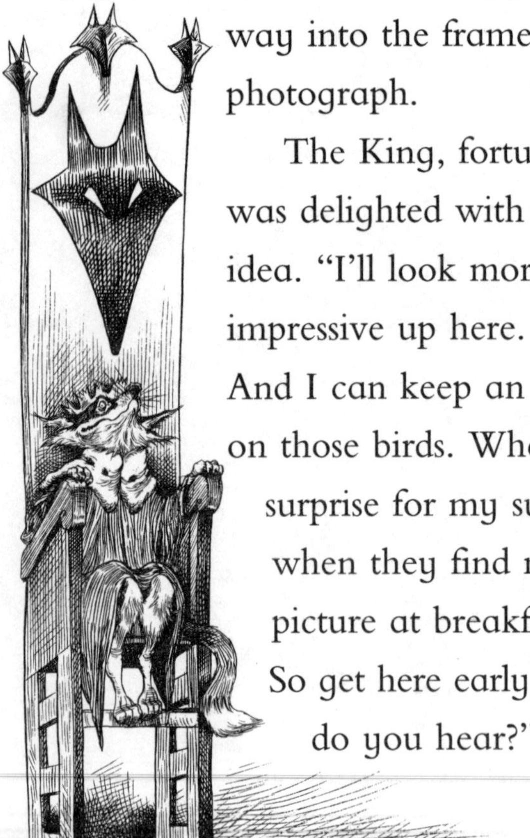

The King, fortunately, was delighted with the idea. "I'll look more impressive up here. And I can keep an eye on those birds. What a surprise for my subjects when they find my new picture at breakfast, right? So get here early, monkey, do you hear?"

When the exhausted monkey dragged himself home, his fingers hurting from the terrible liquid, the latest photograph of the King had just been plastered on the front door of his house. Just at that moment a soldier was leaving.

"No cause for alarm, Mr Monkey," the soldier laughed. "Just a routine inspection to see if anybody is sabotaging His Wolfhood's pictures."

The Monkey rushed inside. "Our daughter? Is she all right? Did she say anything?"

"I'm fine, Dad," the little girl said. "Those wolves are gone, aren't they? And you brought me that special photo – you know, the one I asked you for?"

The monkey felt as if from all four walls, from all four pictures on the four walls, the eight eyes of the Biggest of Wolves were watching each word he might say.

"Let your father rest," said her mother. "The only pictures he's taken are the ones we've put up in the house, like good citizens."

But the next morning, the monkey was awakened by his child's kiss. She put her lips near his ears and whispered something so softly that only he could hear it: "Thank you. It's the best present you could ever give me. You're a magical dad."

"Thanks? Thanks for what?"

She motioned almost imperceptibly toward the wall from which the photo of the Wolf King ruled. Her father opened his eyes wide. In one of the corners of that picture, like the sun rising over the mountains, he could just glimpse, in the act of making their gradual but glorious appearance, a pair of, yes, of course, a pair of soft, pink, pointed ears.

The monkey jumped out of bed. The liquid he had applied did not work permanently. The rabbits had needed the whole night to sneak back into the pictures, but somehow they had managed it.

"I think they knew I was scared," the little girl murmured, "and came to see me while I slept."

Her father dressed in less time than it takes a chill to run up a spine and scurried to the palace without stopping for breakfast. Was this happening only at their house or could the same invasion have taken place everywhere in the kingdom? If so, how could the rabbits be removed from so many portraits?

His Wolfishness was still in bed, but the counsellor was already pacing about, biting the tip of his tail. "It's a plague," he said, "but, fortunately, it is already under control. The offending pictures have been burned. As for you . . ."

"I swear that I—"

"Not a word from you," interrupted the fox. "It's lucky those creatures don't exist. Imagine the damage they'd cause if they really existed. But enough talk. What we need now is a new photo to replace the ones that are contaminated."

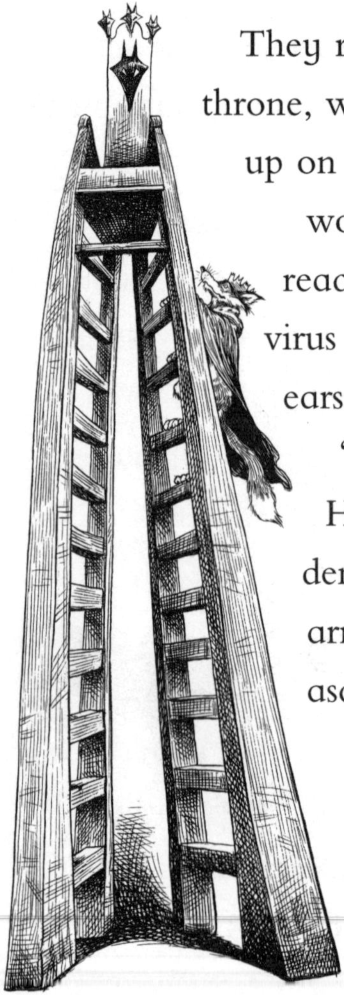

They rushed to the new throne, which was now set up on the top of colossal wooden legs, out of reach of the spreading virus of the mischievous ears.

"I want two shots," His Wolfhood demanded when he arrived, "one of me ascending my throne and another of me sitting on it, enjoying the fresh air. And send them abroad too, so those silly foreign papers will stop attacking me."

This time, when the photos were developed, there was no trouble. Not so much as a carrot of a sign of a rabbit.

"Didn't I tell you? Didn't I tell you they don't exist?" The counsellor was jubilant. "It was just a matter of you focusing the camera properly."

For the next few days, there were no more unpleasant surprises.

The Wolf of Wolves felt happy, high above the heads of the multitude. He let his lieutenants run things while he posed for pictures giving

commands, delivering speeches, signing laws. He examined the shots carefully, however. "Congratulations," he said. "You're being more careful, monkey. It seems you're learning your trade just by being near me. I don't see any more of those whitish spots that spoiled my first pictures."

But one morning, the monkey was again awakened by his daughter's voice. "They're back, Dad," she whispered in his ear. "Those pictures you took are magical."

In one set of photos, at the foot of the towering throne, a small army of rabbits was biting, chewing and splintering the wooden legs. Their teeth worked patiently, and they stopped their work only now and again to wave to the spectators.

The counsellor was

waiting. The monkey could see his fur ruffling and swelling like a swarm of bees.

"How many this time?" the monkey asked.

"The photos are being taken care of," the fox said grimly. "But the birds have got wind of what happened, and now they're telling everyone that those . . . those awful animals exist. And His Wolfinity is beginning to suspect something. 'Why are those birds so happy, so shrill?' he asks. I told him they're just a bunch of featherbrains, full of hot air."

"What did he answer?" asked the monkey.

The King had announced that balloons are full of hot air too and that they could be popped. If those birds didn't keep quiet, he'd make them disappear, just like those unmentionable furry creatures.

But the counsellor had another idea: the Wolf of All Wolves should tie a recording of one of his latest speeches around the necks of the birds. They would have to carry not only the photos, but also the King's words, all over his kingdom. Nobody would be able to hear any of their songs.

"Hearing is believing," trumpeted His Wolfiness. "We'll give them a taste of some hymns, some military marches, some lessons in history, economics and ethics."

The old monkey's life became unbearable. Not even the recorded howls of the King and his chorus of warlike beasts could stop the timid appearance, in the next photo, of an inquisitive nose, a pair of furry ears, some white whiskers, and something hungry gnawing away at the legs of the throne.

The fox replaced the chief officer of the royal guard with a boa constrictor straight from the jungle of a neighbouring country. He put small, hundred-eyed spiders in strategic places throughout the Wolfdom. One day he ordered half the population to shave off their shiny fur so that no spy could hide in it. To punish the cows, accused of uttering subversive moos, he commanded that their milk be soured. And finally, he raised the volume of the King's broadcasts. But in spite of these efforts, there began to be heard a persistent, rowdy, merry sound, the clicking of thousands of tiny teeth, the burbling of an underground stream.

The monkey felt dizzy.

The rhythm was maddening. During the night, the legs of the throne, spindlier by the minute, were reinforced grudgingly by woodpeckers who would have much preferred to take the throne apart. The monkey had to rely on every photographic trick of the trade, now erasing, now trimming with scissors, disguising ears so they looked like shadows and shadows so they looked like wallpaper. He even began using old portraits of the King, trying to make them seem like recent ones.

Until one night, when it was very late, the old monkey was awakened by an angry hand that shook him from his slumber. It was the counsellor, flanked by a fierce escort of soldiers. The Lord Wolf had sent for him.

The whole house was up by now. The little girl watched her father begin dressing.

"Say hello to His Foxcellency," said the monkey.

"Dad," she said, and it was astonishing that she did not speak in a low, fearful voice anymore, as if the armed guards were not even there, "today you've got to bring me that picture I asked for."

"A picture?" The counsellor showed

interest. "A picture of what, of whom?"

The child continued to ignore him. "Today you'll bring me a photo of the rabbits, right, Dad? For my wall?"

The mother monkey touched the girl's head as if she had a fever. "Hasn't your father told you that rabbits don't exist? Haven't we shut you up in your room for telling lies?"

"They exist," the little girl announced.

"Everybody knows they exist."

"Just as I suspected," said the counsellor. "Let's go."

The Wolfiest of Wolves was waiting for them atop his throne. Around each leg, hundreds of guards and snakes kept watch.

"Monkey, you are a traitor," thundered the King. "Your photos are being used by people who say that strange and malicious creatures – who are non-existent as everyone knows – are conspiring this very night to overthrow my rule. They say my throne trembles and my dynasty will topple. Is there any evidence that my throne trembles? Does

anybody dare say so?" And he yowled like a hundred jet fighters in the air. "We'll start by making a recording of that sound. And you, you monkey, you're going to help me stamp out these rumours. Touching is believing. You are going to make me a wide-angle, three-dimensional picture that will cover all walls. In colour. Because I am going to crown myself Emperor of the Wolves, the Supreme Wolferor. And if a single wretched rabbit shows its snout, I will make you eat the photos, one by one, a million of them, and then I'll eat you and not only you, but your wife and your daughter, and all the monkeys in this country. Now. Take that picture."

The monkey stuck his quaking head under the black cloth behind his camera and focused on the throne. He let out a little moan. Up till then, the rabbits had appeared only later, when the picture was developed. But here they were now, directly in front of his lens, ungovernable and carefree, gnawing away, biting not only the wood of the throne, but also the swords of the astonished guards and the very rattles of the rattlesnakes.

"What's the matter?" bellowed the future Wolferor, who was not looking downward so his profile would be perfect for posterity.

The monkey moved the camera nearer the throne, hoping the rabbit army would not appear in the picture. The rabbits moved faster than he did. They were clambering up the legs, one on top of the other as if they were monkeys or birds. The soldiers tried to frighten them away in silence, unwilling to attract the attention of the King, but the invaders were too agile. The Wolves kept bumping into one another and hitting each other over the head.

The monkey realized that a contingent of birds had arrived from above, winging freely through the air, without a cord tied to them or a recording.

"Hurry up!" ordered the Wolf of all Wolves.

The monkey closed his eyes very tightly. It was better not to witness what

was going to happen. At
the very moment that
he clicked the shutter,
he heard a deafening
noise. He knew
what he was going
to see when he
opened his eyes, but
still could not believe
it: like an old elm
tree rotten to the
core, the throne
had come
crashing to the
ground along
with the King

of Wolves, guards, snakes, counsellor, and all. The monkey blinked. There at the foot of his tripod lay the Biggest, Baddest, the Most Boastful Wolf in the Universe. His ribs were broken, his black fur was torn by the fall, his yellow eyes were reddened, and he was wailing in pain.

"Monkey," squeaked the would-be Wolferer of the World, "this picture . . . you have my permission not to publish it."

At that moment, all the lights in the palace went out. The monkey was paralyzed. He did not know where to go. Then, as if someone in the darkness were suddenly shining a light on a pathway, he knew what he must do. He grabbed his camera and his bag, and clutching them to his chest like a treasure, he fled.

His daughter was waiting for him at the door of the house.

"Wait," he said to her. "Wait. I've brought you something." And without another word, he raced into his darkroom to develop the last picture as quickly as possible.

When he came out a few minutes later, his daughter and wife were standing on chairs, taking down the pictures of the Wolf King.

"Here," the old monkey said to his daughter, blinking in the bright light. "Here, this is the picture you've been asking for all this time. I've finally brought you your present."

"Thanks, Dad," the little girl said. "But I don't need it anymore."

She pointed around the room and toward the street and across the fields where the sun was beginning to rise.

The world was full of rabbits.